"**W**here are we going? And what is this tunnel?" you ask. "You said that no one else knows about it. Is that really true?"

Ramses laughs. "There are many tunnels through the pyramid. Only I know them all. The plans for the inside of the pyramid were changed several times during the building. Many tunnels were left as they were when they made new ones. Tunnels were made for the workmen to get air and to escape when the ceremonial tunnels were sealed with tons of stone. They never filled in the tunnels of the workmen."

"That was dumb," you say. "The tomb robbers could use them to get to the pharaoh's treasure and—"

"They would never find their way out. These tunnels are like a maze. You want to try? Look behind you."

You turn, but when you turn back, Ramses is gone.

"Ramses, come back!" you shout. The sound of your voice echoes through the tunnels.

You try to find your way out, but you are trapped inside the Great Pyramid. What will you do?

**ONLY *YOU*, AS YOUNG INDIANA JONES,
CAN DECIDE...**

Bantam Books in the Choose Your Own Adventure® series
Ask your bookseller for the books you have missed

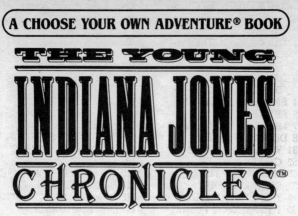

THE YOUNG INDIANA JONES CHRONICLES™

Book 1

THE VALLEY OF THE KINGS

EGYPT, May 1908

By Richard Brightfield

Adapted from the television movie
"Young Indiana Jones and the Curse of
the Jackal"
Teleplay by Jonathan Hales
Story by George Lucas

Illustrated by Frank Bolle

BANTAM BOOKS

NEW YORK · TORONTO · LONDON · SYDNEY · AUCKLAND

RL 5, age 10 and up

THE VALLEY OF THE KINGS
A Bantam Book / July 1992

CHOOSE YOUR OWN ADVENTURE® is a registered trademark of Bantam Books, a division of Bantam Doubleday Dell Publishing Group, Inc. Registered in U.S. Patent and Trademark Office and elsewhere. Original conception of Edward Packard

THE YOUNG INDIANA JONES CHRONICLES™
is a trademark of Lucasfilm Ltd. All rights reserved. Used under authorization.

*Cover art by George Tsui
Interior Illustrations by Frank Bolle*

*All rights reserved.
Copyright © 1992 by Lucasfilm Ltd.*

ISBN 0-553-29756-2

Published simultaneously in the United States and Canada

Bantam Books are published by Bantam Books, a division of Bantam Doubleday Dell Publishing Group, Inc. Its trademark, consisting of the words "Bantam Books" and the portrayal of a rooster, is Registered in U.S. Patent and Trademark Office and in other countries. Marca Registrada. Bantam Books, 666 Fifth Avenue, New York, New York 10103.

PRINTED IN THE UNITED STATES OF AMERICA
OPM 0 9 8 7 6 5 4 3 2 1

THE VALLEY OF THE KINGS

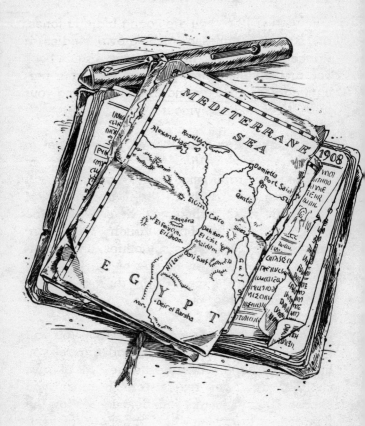

Your Adventure

The year is 1908. You are young Indiana Jones, the son of a professor of medieval studies at Princeton University in New Jersey. In this book you are traveling through Egypt with your parents, Professor Henry and Anna Jones, and your tutor, Miss Helen Seymour.

In the adventures that follow, you will get to meet many famous figures in history, such as Lawrence of Arabia and Howard Carter. You will also experience firsthand life in ancient Egypt and learn about archeology, the secrets of the pyramids, the curse of the pharaohs, the ancient language of hieroglyphs, mummies, and the afterlife. You may even be one of the lucky explorers who are present at the discovery of an ancient pharaoh's tomb!

From time to time as you read along, you will be asked to make a choice. The adventures you have as Indiana Jones are the results of your choices. You are responsible because you choose. After you make your decision, follow the instructions to find out what happens to you next. Remember, your Egyptian adventures depend on the actions you decide to take.

To help you in your travels, a special glossary is provided at the end of the book.

You are Indiana Jones. You were born in 1899 in Princeton, New Jersey, where your father is a professor of medieval studies at the university. It is now 1908, and you are eight years old. At the moment, you are on an ocean liner steaming from England to Egypt, where your father is to give a series of lectures at the University of Cairo. Also along on the trip are your mother, Anna, and Helen Seymour, the tutor your father hired for you back in England.

You are not too happy about having a tutor. Ever since Miss Seymour arrived she's been drilling you mercilessly on your studies. You are forced to spend most of your time in a tiny cabin crammed with books and teaching equipment.

The ship suddenly pitches violently, sending books and papers flying. Miss Seymour grabs hold of the edge of the small desk to keep her balance. Somehow you manage to suppress a laugh. When the ship levels off, Miss Seymour looks at her watch.

"I see it's time for dinner," she says. "Button up your suit, we're dining with the captain tonight."

→ → → → → → → → → → → →
Turn to page 2.

2

You hate the stiff English schoolboy's suit that Miss Seymour has forced you to wear, but you button it up and follow her out onto the deserted deck, bracing yourself against the wind. Up ahead, a huge wave breaks over the bow of the ship, and a few seconds later, you are showered with spray.

Somehow you and Miss Seymour make it forward to the ship's dining room. Your mother and father are there, sitting on one side of a large table.

"How about sitting over here next to me?" your father asks you. "Maybe after dinner I can get a progress report on your studies."

Several others, including the captain, are seated around the table. These include an elderly bishop and a middle-aged husband and wife. Everyone except your father and the captain looks a bit green from the weather.

Just as you are sitting down, the ship lurches, and you nearly tumble over.

"Heavy weather, eh Captain!" the bishop says.

"A bit lively. I hope it's not spoiling your enjoyment of the voyage," the captain says.

"We're a hardy island breed, we Englishmen," the bishop says. "Salty sea dogs and all that."

The ship lurches violently again as the captain looks over at you.

"How are your studies progressing?" he asks.

"Fine, thank you, sir," you say.

"And what did you learn about today?"

"About mummies, sir."

"Mummies?" the captain says.

"About how the ancient Egyptians turned people into mummies—uh, after they died," you add.

"Really! And how did they go about that?" the captain asks, looking at Miss Seymour with a knowing glance.

"Well, first they drove a tube up through the nose into the brain and poured in chemicals that would soften it up," you say. "Then they scooped out the brain."

A gasp goes around the table.

→ → → → → → → → → → → → →

Go on to the next page.

"They pulled it out through the nose using a metal fork," you go on, demonstrating by holding the end of your fork to your nose. "And then they—"

"That's quite enough," your mother interrupts.

"But Mom, this is interesting," you say. "I thought you wanted me to learn."

"And then?" your father asks with a wry look of amusement.

The middle-aged couple gets up and leaves, saying they want to catch up on their reading before going to bed early.

"The next part was great, Dad," you say. "They cut open the left side of the corpse, reached in, and yanked out most of the lower organs. Then they cut the chest open and pulled out everything except the heart. They washed all the organs in salt, then poured some kind of hot goo over them."

"Since you insist on allowing this to go on, I'm leaving," your mother says to your father, getting up from the table and heading for the door.

You look over at Miss Seymour and notice that she has turned pale. That's strange, you think, she's the one who made me read about all this. You go on with your description.

→ → → → → → → → → → → →

Go on to the next page.

"They packed the body with salt, then sewed it up again, plugging up the nose and sticking bits of cloth under the eyelids," you continue.

Miss Seymour puts down her fork and leaves with as much dignity as she can. "If you'll excuse me," she manages to say.

"Most of the mummies leaked," you say, "and—"

The captain slowly rises. He, too, looks pretty green. "I believe I'm wanted on the bridge."

"That was quite a speech," your father says. "Now finish your tripe before it's completely cold."

Tripe? That's what this strange-tasting stuff is, you think, looking down at the food on your plate. You remember reading that it's made from the lining of a cow's stomach.

Suddenly you don't feel too well yourself. Every time the ship heaves from side to side, your stomach seems to go with it. You wish your father hadn't mentioned the tripe.

"If you'll excuse me, I think I'll go on deck," you say, getting to your feet.

"Are you feeling all right?" your father asks. "You look a little green around the gills, if you don't mind my saying so."

You just nod and stagger to the door of the dining room.

Outside, the cool salt air makes you feel better for a moment, but only for a moment. Luckily you make it to the ship's railing before you lose your dinner over the side.

Still weak, you manage to make it back to your stateroom. Inside, Miss Seymour is sitting rigidly in a chair in the corner, her arms folded.

"I appreciate your interest in your schoolwork," she says. "But I do think you could have left out some of the more graphic details at dinner."

"Well, isn't that what I'm supposed to be doing, using what I learn and trying to—"

"Very well, then," Miss Seymour interrupts as she pushes herself unsteadily to her feet. "Let's get back to the blackboard and begin where we left off."

The next day, the weather is calmer. The day after, the ocean becomes glassy. The ship, powered by coal and steam, plows on and on.

Miss Seymour's mood, however, never changes for the better. She even steps up your studies. In between lessons, you manage to stand on deck, gazing out over the sea for long stretches of time. Sometimes your father joins you by the railing.

"Are we near Egypt yet?" you ask him.

→ → → → → → → → → → → → →

Go on to the next page.

"We'll enter the Mediterranean through the Strait of Gibraltar late this afternoon," your father explains, "then steam along the north coast of Africa. A few more days and we should be in Alexandria."

"A few days!" you exclaim.

"Just be patient and enjoy the trip," your father says.

Sure, just be patient, you repeat to yourself. At the moment you are completely fed up with Miss Seymour and her endless lessons. You just hope you can resist the temptation to push her overboard before you arrive in Egypt. Once there, maybe you can find a way to escape. On board ship, there's really no place for you to hide.

That night, with the sky overhead clear and brilliant with stars, you watch a long string of thunderstorms prowling the African coast in the far distance. Horizontal bolts of lightning flash in sequence from one side of the otherwise invisible horizon and then back again. The storms are too far away to hear the thunder. Instead the only sound you hear is the steady hiss of the bow wake as the ship continues on its course through the Mediterranean.

A couple of days later, you finally reach the coast of Egypt. The narrow strip of beach in the

distance thickens, and low, sand-colored buildings surrounded by clusters of cranes pointing
skyward come into view as the ship heads into
Alexandria, Egypt's major port.

You, your mother and father, and Miss Seymour assemble on deck, ready to disembark as
the ship docks. The strap of your leather book
bag is slung over your shoulder. The rest of the
luggage will be sent separately to your hotel in
Cairo.

→ → → → → → → → → → → →
Go on to the next page.

As soon as the gangplank is positioned, the four of you start down. The dock itself is crowded with all sorts of people—tall, thin men with beards and turbans, women in print dresses and head scarves, and men in suits wearing red hats that look like flower pots turned upside down. Miss Seymour tells you that these hats are tarbooshes or red fezes. They indicate that the wearers are effendi, or civil servants. Many other people, obviously English, are wearing hats that look like upside-down bowls.

"Those are called pith helmets," Miss Seymour says, pointing them out.

"The people in this place are certainly different," you say.

"The Suez Canal, farther up the coast, is known as the British 'Lifeline of the Empire,'" Miss Seymour says. "It brings India six thousand miles closer to England. People are here from all over the world. They say that the sun never sets on the British Empire—and they're right. Its possessions are strung out around the globe: Egypt, India, Australia, South Africa, and Canada, not to mention Hong Kong and scores of other islands. I'm told that the Empire holds one-quarter of the world's land and a fourth of its people."

"Wow!" you say, impressed.

→ → → → → → → → → → → →

Go on to the next page.

You get to the bottom of the gangplank and start toward the line of horse-drawn carriages at the end of the pier.

Your parents lead the way through the crowd, with Miss Seymour close behind them and you bringing up the rear.

Suddenly you feel a tug at your shoulder from behind. You turn just in time to see a small boy running off with your book bag. Besides your textbooks, it contains all the notes you've made during the trip.

You have a split second to decide. You can either call to Helen and your parents for help, or you can chase after the thief yourself.

→   →   →   →   →   →   →   →   →   →   →   →

If you decide to call to your parents,
turn to page 72.

If you decide to chase after the thief yourself,
turn to page 111.

You decide to stay and see Carter open the tomb. Rashid can appreciate your curiosity, but he reluctantly leaves to scout out the Valley of the Kings as he was instructed to do.

"Are we going inside now?" you ask.

"In a moment," Carter says. "First, I have to make sure that our photographer has recorded the murals inside the first chamber." Carter calls over to a man lugging out a heavy box camera mounted on a tripod. "Pierre, did you have enough light in the tomb for your camera?"

"*Certainement* . . . ah, certainly" Pierre says, leaving his equipment and coming over to your group. "I set up a large mirror just outside the entrance to reflect the sunlight inside. I left it there so that you would have plenty of light yourself."

"Thank you," Carter says. "I'll take my young friend here inside now. This will be a real introduction for you to the science of archeology," he tells you.

"Are you looking for buried treasure inside the tomb?" you ask.

Carter laughs. "I hope to find something. However, all indications suggest that this tomb has been cleaned out by robbers. The door to the inner chamber is a makeshift one from a later date. Originally it was blocked with stones and mud plaster."

→ → → → → → → → → → → → →

Go on to the next page.

14

Carter enters the tomb, followed by you, Lawrence, and Lord Carnarvon. The light from Pierre's mirror illuminates the room. The walls are covered with beautiful murals, painted in full color.

"Look here on this wall," Carter says. "The artist has illustrated what happens to you after death."

"Really!" you say, shuddering at the thought.

→ → → → → → → → → → → →

Turn to page 73.

The train whistle blows several times, and then the train begins to move slowly and smoothly. Soon it picks up speed and leaves the city behind, breaking out into a broad, flat landscape of green, cultivated fields.

This unchanging scenery whizzes by for hours, then abruptly changes to a vast suburb of innumerable tiny, tightly packed mud brick houses. The narrow alleys between them are crowded with donkeys, goats, and brown-skinned children. Up ahead, in the distance, you see a wall of massive buildings with dozens of ornate minarets rising above it. Soon you are there. The train, with a loud hiss of steam, comes to a stop in the station.

A horse-drawn carriage then takes you slowly through the crowded streets of Cairo, streets filled—like Alexandria—with people and animals of all kinds. Tall, beardless black men wearing elaborate headdresses and multicolored robes wrapped around them like Roman togas rub shoulders with Europeans in business suits and pith helmets, as well as Egyptian officials wearing red fezes. Others, with olive complexions and full beards, are wearing turbans and military uniforms. In addition, there are delicately boned natives with faces black as coal dressed in spotless robes of white cotton.

"Those costumes are called galabiyas," Miss Seymour says.

→ → → → → → → → → → → → →

Go on to the next page.

The pedestrians share the streets with groups of camels being herded along and donkey carts of all sizes—some full of cages with pigs or chickens, others piled high with vegetables.

Finally you arrive at the hotel, an ornate, multistoried building. Your carriage joins a long line of other carriages lined up in front. Several porters rush out to unload your steamer trunks from the carriage that has been accompanying yours.

You, Miss Seymour, and your parents get out, go up the front steps of the hotel, and step out onto a broad terrace. You pass a row of waiters dressed in crimson jackets with gold trimming and loose-fitting white pants—all standing at attention. Opposite them, several dozen elegantly dressed Europeans are chatting at café tables scattered in a miniature forest of potted palms.

An oversized door leads you into the broad, carpeted lobby. Overhead, hanging from the high ceiling, is an enormous chandelier made of thousands of small pieces of cut crystal. Your mother and father go over to one side and confer with the hotel manager.

"This is *some* place!" you say to Miss Seymour.

"A playground of the rich," she says distastefully.

"I need to review my notes for the lecture this afternoon," your father says, coming back to where you are standing. "And your mother is

Go on to the next page

going to have her hands full with the social arrangements. I'm—"

"Don't worry about us," Miss Seymour says. "I've prepared an itinerary—things to do that will tie into Indy's studies, of course. However, as a diversion from our more serious investigations, I suggest a trip to one of the markets here in Cairo. We may even buy a few souvenirs, provided they are moderately priced."

"May I suggest the Khan el-Khalili, a most excellent market, or suq as we call it," says the hotel manager, who has just come over to join your group. "I'll arrange for a guide right away."

"A guide?" Miss Seymour says. "We're quite capable of—"

"I think the manager's advice is quite valid," your father interrupts.

"If you insist, Professor Jones," Miss Seymour says reluctantly.

A short time later, you and Miss Seymour leave the hotel. A carriage and a guide are waiting. You climb inside while the guide, a young man wearing a turban but otherwise dressed in Western style, takes a seat opposite you.

After a twenty-minute ride back along the crowded streets, during which time the guide is silent, you go through a massive gate—a high, pointed archway several stories high.

$$\rightarrow \quad \rightarrow \quad \rightarrow \quad \rightarrow \quad \rightarrow \quad \rightarrow \quad \rightarrow \quad \rightarrow \quad \rightarrow \quad \rightarrow \quad \rightarrow \quad \rightarrow$$

Go on to the next page.

"We go through the 'Bab al-Futuh,' The Gate of Conquest," the guide suddenly announces with an accent that seems a mixture of Shakespearian English and Arabic. "Much of the old city is still surrounded by the ancient walls. You see now before you the 'Shari al-Mu'izz,' the main avenue of the old city."

Ahead of you stretches a wide street with massive buildings rising on either side. The guide points out some of them as your carriage moves slowly against the usual tide of people and animals.

"Over there is the citadel built by Saladin, the general who led the Muslim forces against the crusaders in the twelfth century," he says. "And beside it is the great mosque of Muhammad Ali, built in the eighteen-twenties. He was the founder of the dynasty that ruled Egypt from the beginning of the nineteenth century to the middle of the twentieth."

You reach another, smaller, but still impressive gate. The carriage stops in front of it and the three of you climb out. The guide leads you through on foot, then into a broad plaza filled with awning-covered stalls piled high with every kind of merchandise imaginable.

"Each kind of goods is sold in its own area," the guide says. "You will enjoy walking around. You go as you wish, I will follow."

You and Miss Seymour take his advice and

start through the crowd, the members of which gesture and shout as they bargain. You notice dozens of coppersmiths sitting there, vigorously hammering patterns into trays. The noise of the voices, combined with the pounding of the coppersmiths, makes an almost deafening sound.

Farther on you come to the fruit market, which has huge piles of vegetables. You thread your way among them on the way to the textile market, where the stalls are piled high with rolls of cotton and silk. This area has a musty smell. Then you approach a section with large trays piled high with different spices.

"How fascinating. I recognize ginger and cardamom," Miss Seymour says, bending over the different trays. "Oh, and these must be cumin, saffron, and coriander."

"I don't know what you call them, but they certainly smell good," you say.

The next is the perfume suq, with a whole new array of smells. Miss Seymour buys a small bottle of sandalwood. This starts a rush of different vendors after her, all beseeching her to buy their products. "I think it's time we got out of here," she says, trying to push her way through the crowd of merchants gathered around her.

Miss Seymour finally breaks free and heads, with you and the guide following, back toward the entrance to the suq.

→ → → → → → → → → → → →

Go on to the next page.

Then, off to one side, you hear a completely different sound—the music of a flute.

"What's going on?" you ask the guide.

He laughs. "A snake charmer, I believe."

"Can we go see?" you ask Miss Seymour. "Maybe we can get through the crowd."

"Well . . . all right," she says reluctantly. "We can try. But let's stay close together."

You head in that direction. The crowd parts for a few seconds, and you catch sight of the snake charmer and the snake. It's a cobra, swaying back and forth to the sound of a flute. Miss Seymour tells you that the snake is actually following the body movement of the flutist.

Then the crowd closes in again, and you lose sight of the snake, as well as your guide and Miss Seymour, as you are pushed sideways. You realize that this is your chance to slip away into the crowd and escape from Miss Seymour for a while. You'll have a perfect excuse later—the crowd carried you away and you got lost. On the other hand, the scene is somewhat frenetic. Perhaps you should stay with Miss Seymour and your guide. You have to make your decision now. You have only a few seconds before they find you again.

→　→　→　→　→　→　→　→　→　→　→　→

If you decide to sneak away into the crowd, turn to page 79.

If you decide to stay with Miss Seymour and the guide, turn to page 48.

"I think I'd better turn in and get some rest," you say. "I'm kinda worn out from climbing the pyramid."

Lawrence nods, then goes into the farmhouse and comes back with two woolen blankets, one for you and one for Miss Seymour. "You'd better use these," he says. "It can get quite chilly out here during the night. Oh, and don't worry, you'll be quite safe here. My friends will look after the two of you. I'll be back later."

You just barely hear him say this as you drift off to sleep by the fire.

→ → → → → → → → → → → →

Turn to page 49.

Sometime later, after creeping through the usual traffic, you cross a bridge over the Nile. The river shimmers in the heat, and for the first time, you can see the peaks of the pyramids rising out of a dusty haze far to the southwest.

The carriage goes on for another ten minutes, then stops in front of a stable. You and Miss Seymour get out.

"What is your fee, and that of the driver?" Miss Seymour asks the guide somewhat warily.

"Both compliments of the hotel, madam."

"Oh, really?" Miss Seymour says. "That's nice of them." However, she does tip them both a piaster. From the look on her face as she does, you can tell it's painful for her. What an old skinflint, you think.

You and Miss Seymour walk over to the stable where you can find a camel driver who speaks English. She proceeds to bargain for two camels. The driver leads the camels out, and at a command from him, they crouch on the ground with their legs folded. You climb up on one while Miss Seymour, with the help of the driver, climbs onto the other.

→ → → → → → → → → → → →

Go on to the next page.

The driver shouts another command, and your camel then rises in a series of violent lurches that almost throw you off. You look over and see Miss Seymour hanging on grimly as hers does the same.

With the driver leading on foot, your camels start off and head along a broad, elevated roadway.

The pyramids get larger and larger as you approach them. As you get nearer, they seem to be hovering over you. Somehow they make you feel very tiny and insignificant. At the base of the largest pyramid the camels come to a stop, and the mounting process is reversed as the camels kneel in another series of lurches.

Almost immediately, several would-be guides rush over. Miss Seymour, however, is engaged in a heated discussion with the camel driver over the fee for the trip.

"You wait right here until we come back," you hear her say.

After that, Miss Seymour selects a guide—the one who seems to speak the best English. You can tell that she would rather the two of you climb the pyramid alone, but she gives in, realizing that the situation is hopeless.

→ → → → → → → → → → → → →

Go on to the next page.

You start up the pyramid, following the guide. The going is not as easy as you thought it would be. You have to climb over large stones, many of them three or four feet high. You look back down and see the camel driver glaring up at you and Miss Seymour. He's shaking his fist.

"Miss Seymour," you say. "The driver seems mad at us."

"Just a bit peeved, I expect. I gave him ten piasters and he wanted thirty."

"Ten piasters. Is that a lot?" you ask.

"It's entirely sufficient," she says. "These people expect to barter. It's part of their nature. You'll see, by the time we get down he'll be perfectly content, and more than glad to take us back."

"I hope so," you say. "He looks awfully mad."

After another ten minutes of climbing, the guide announces, "We stop here a moment, explain few things about pyramid. The pyramid you are climbing is world's largest stone structure. Made of two million stone blocks, most weighing two and a half tons. It was constructed over four thousand years ago by the pharaoh Khufu. Inside is burial chamber where his body was originally laid to rest—he hoped for eternity."

"I think we already know about that, don't we?" Miss Seymour says to you. "That is, if you studied all your lessons on the ship as you were supposed to."

"I remember all those things, including that some of the pharaohs were very old when they finished their pyramids. Ramses II was over ninety."

"And don't forget that some were your age," Miss Seymour says.

You try to remember your lessons. Now that you're climbing one of the great pyramids—the greatest, actually—everything is slowly coming back to you.

"Some believe that shape of pyramid symbolizes the rays of the sun descending to earth," the guide continues.

→ → → → → → → → → → → →
Go on to the next page.

The guide's voice is gradually drowned out by the beat of drums and the clashing of a thousand tambourines as a vision forms before your eyes— a vision of *you* as pharaoh. You imagine yourself held aloft on a gilded platform, carried on the shoulders of a dozen of your nobles.

You wear the tall double crown representing the union of upper and lower Egypt. On either side of you, attendants wave huge fans of ostrich feathers on the ends of silver poles to keep you cool.

The sound of trumpets and the beat of horses' hooves announce the arrival of the war chariots as they pass in review in front of you. The heads and tails of their horses are decorated with multi-colored plumes. Foot soldiers follow in formation, the tips of their spears glinting in the sun. Archers jog by, their long bows slung over their shoulders and sheaves of arrows in their hands.

The army is followed by a great procession of white-robed priests and priestesses, all singing a hymn to your glory.

Suddenly there is a shrilling of a hundred flutes. Down a broad avenue decorated with flowers, the entire assembly, stretching as far as you can see, prostrates itself before you.

At this moment, Miss Seymour shakes you by the shoulder and breaks the spell of your daydream. "We're starting up again," she says.

→ → → → → → → → → → → →

Go on to the next page.

"Over to the right," the guide says, "are the two other pyramids of Giza. The closest one, built by Khufu's son, Kheophren, is slightly smaller than this one, but as you can see, it still has some of the original limestone cap.

"And way over there to the left is the much smaller pyramid built by Khufu's grandson, Menkaru. Down below, you can see the Sphinx, the huge, human-headed statue of a lion. It guards the end of the original ceremonial causeway, now gone, that once led to Kheophren's pyramid. The features of the Sphinx are believed to be those of Kheophren himself."

The guide goes on and on. You know a lot of this stuff already from your studies, and you're waiting for something exciting to happen.

The guide starts up again, and you reach a large opening dug into the side of the pyramid. A crowd of tourists is gathered around it.

"Here's where we go into the pyramid itself and see the actual burial chamber of the pharaoh," the guide says.

"I'd rather keep going to the top," Miss Seymour says. "It's getting late, and I want to get up and back down before dark. We can see the burial chamber some other time. I'm not even sure I want to—"

"But madam," the guide pleads, "the Grand Gallery leading to the burial chamber is magnificent and not to be missed. The chamber itself

contains the pharaoh's huge granite sarcophagus."

"I don't care..." Miss Seymour starts. She and
the guide get into a big argument. The crowd
gathers around to listen.

"Psssst." A sound comes from behind you. You
turn and see a small, barefoot boy in a tattered
galabiya.

"Want to see a secret passage in the pyramid?"
he whispers. "I'm the only one who knows where
it is."

A secret passage! you think. That sounds interesting. Miss Seymour is so involved in her argument that it would be easy to slip away. You can rejoin her later—she might still be arguing when you get back. On the other hand, you don't really know where this boy could be leading you. Maybe you should wait and just keep going up the pyramid.

→ → → → → → → → → → → → →

If you decide to take the boy up on his offer, turn to page 87.

If you decide to wait for Miss Seymour, turn to page 57.

You decide to go with Lawrence upriver by dhow. Early the next morning, you take a carriage from the hotel to a dock area along the river. You are carrying a new canvas bag with some new textbooks and some extra clothing, as well as a large picnic basket your mother has packed with food from the hotel kitchen.

Lawrence is waiting for you at the foot of a pier that stretches out into the Nile. You follow him to the other end, where a large wooden boat sits low in the water. There are no cabins, just a wide, flat deck piled with cargo, from which two tall masts point skyward.

"Doesn't this look like something out of the *Arabian Nights*?" Lawrence asks.

You nod, then the two of you jump on board the boat.

$\rightarrow \quad \rightarrow \quad \rightarrow \quad \rightarrow \quad \rightarrow \quad \rightarrow \quad \rightarrow \quad \rightarrow \quad \rightarrow \quad \rightarrow \quad \rightarrow \quad \rightarrow$

Go on to the next page.

"Just find a comfortable place to plant yourself and relax," Lawrence says. "We'll be setting sail in a few minutes."

You climb over some cargo and find a big coil of thick rope to sit on. Overhead, the sailors, some holding the hems of their galabiyas in their teeth to keep from tripping, are climbing up the masts to unfurl the large cotton sails. On the pier, along the length of the fifty-foot boat, ropes are being cast off. Soon the dhow is floating free in the river. The sails catch a slight breeze, and the boat moves offshore with surprising speed.

→ → → → → → → → → → → → →

Turn to page 59.

You are three-quarters of the way down when you notice something far below. "Miss Seymour, look!" you say.

"Oh, my goodness! The camel driver is taking our camels away."

"Hey, wait!" you call out. But the driver, now riding one of the camels, continues to gallop off, leading the other camel with a long rope.

Fifteen minutes later, you are finally all the way down the side of the pyramid. But the driver and his camels are now completely out of sight.

"What do we do now?" you ask. "Do you think we could walk back?"

"No, it's much too far," Miss Seymour says. "And it's almost dark. We'd never find our way."

"But we can't stay here. What if we're attacked by robbers during the night?"

"Nonsense!"

"But there's no one around. We're sitting ducks," you say.

Miss Seymour grabs you by the arm. "Listen," she says. "There's nothing to be afraid of."

"Look!" you say, pointing to the west where a distant figure is silhouetted against the last glow of sunset. "Someone's coming to murder us."

"Highly unlikely," Miss Seymour says. But you can see, even in the fading light, that she has turned slightly pale.

→ → → → → → → → → → → →

Go on to the next page.

As the ominous figure gets closer, it becomes clear that it is someone riding a bicycle—someone wearing a lightweight suit and a scarf wrapped around his head.

The man stops a short distance away and waves. Then he gets off the bicycle and unwraps his scarf. He's a blond young man with gray eyes, probably twenty years old. He looks quizzically at Miss Seymour.

"Hello there," he says. "My name is T. E. Lawrence. My friends call me Ned. You look awfully familiar."

"I'm Helen Seymour. We met at Oxford, I believe."

"By Jove! I remember now. At a lecture on Persian poetry. And this is . . . ?"

Miss Seymour introduces you. She tells Ned you're from Princeton, New Jersey, back in the States.

"You're not by chance related to *the* Henry Jones, professor of medieval history?"

"My father."

"Then you're a lucky one. His books are brilliant. I've read them all."

"Miss Seymour here is my tutor."

"Then you're doubly lucky, I'd say. And what brings you to such an unlikely spot at this hour?"

"We had a slight misunderstanding with our camel driver—he ran off with them," you explain.

"They will do that," Lawrence says. "But don't worry. There'll be plenty of camels here by morning."

"We can't just sit here all night," Miss Seymour says.

"Quite right. You'd be sure to catch cold, for one thing. The desert can get awfully chilly at night," Lawrence says.

"Then what do we do?" Miss Seymour asks.

"No problem there. I know a family of fellahin farmers, who live nearby. In fact, I was on my way there when I saw you."

"Your parents will be worried sick," Miss Seymour says aloud, more to herself than to you or Lawrence. "They'll never forgive me."

It is now dark except for the light of the stars, which, in the clear night air of the desert, are brighter than you ever thought they could be. The pyramids are tall, black shadows against the stars. Lawrence is a moving shadow himself, pushing his bike in front as you follow.

Soon, the dim shape of a one-story building appears. When you get closer, you see that it's surrounded by a windowless wall with a closed gate at the center.

Lawrence pounds on the gate and calls out in Arabic. An answering cry comes from the other side, and the gate swings open.

→ → → → → → → → → → → → →

Go on to the next page.

"Ahlan wa sahlan," a voice says in the darkness.

"My friend bids us welcome," Lawrence says.

You follow him through the gate and into a courtyard. Sitting around a small fire, several men are wearing tight caps and long galabiyas, the firelight flickering on their faces. Lawrence talks with them in Arabic.

"They hope you will eat some of their humble food," Lawrence says.

One of the men goes into the house behind the courtyard, reappearing with a large copper tray—the kind you saw being made in the suq. Thin, round loaves of bread are piled in the center of it, and small bowls have been placed around the edge. You watch Lawrence as he tears off a piece of the bread and uses it to scoop out some of the contents of one of the bowls. You do the same. It tastes pretty good.

"The spread is called hummus," Lawrence says. "It's made from ground chickpeas."

You and Miss Seymour sit around with the men, silently eating for a while. The only sound is the gentle crackling of the fire.

"It's really amazing, meeting you here like this," Miss Seymour says, breaking the silence.

"I've been up in Syria, looking at the Crusader castles. Before going home I thought I'd visit an archeologist friend of mine working here in Egypt. And you?"

→　→　→　→　→　→　→　→　→　→　→　→

Go on to the next page.

"We came with Professor Jones," Miss Seymour replies. "He's on a lecture tour. Today we came out to see the pyramids."

"And what did you think of them?"

"Oh, very impressive," Miss Seymour says. "Of course I realize that they are just the bare bones of the really amazing tombs they must have once been."

"Tombs, yes," Lawrence says. "But I think they were more than that. They were the focus of the ancient Egyptian religion, rather like the great cathedrals of medieval Europe."

"I know all about the mummies," you interject. "Miss Seymour has been teaching me, and—"

"Let's not go through all that again," Miss Seymour says with a groan, remembering the earlier incident at dinner on the boat coming over from England.

"I just wonder why they went to all that trouble with the corpses, then just buried them under all that rock," you say.

"The ancient Egyptians, as you should know from your studies," Miss Seymour says, "believed that life after death was a continuation of their life when they were alive. It was important that the body be preserved and protected as a home for the *ka*, or 'soul.' All the things one would need for the afterlife were buried with you. Also, the undying spirit needed constant nourishment through eternity in the form of real or symbolic offerings from future relatives. Another part of the spirit, the *ba*, could travel out of the tomb, right through its stone walls, and roam around during the day, returning to the body at night."

"What if the body was destroyed—I mean by tomb robbers, for example?" you ask.

"The Egyptians knew that could happen," she says. "As a backup, they placed realistic statues in secret rooms to which the spirit could return if necessary."

"Is any of that stuff about the spirits true?" you ask.

"Hardly," she says. "But it's what the ancient Egyptians believed."

"I wonder what really happens when you die?" you ask.

"May I quote from one of my favorite poets?" Lawrence asks.

"Please do," Miss Seymour says.

"Strange, is it not? that of the myriads who
Before us pass'd the door of Darkness through,
    Not one returns to tell us of the Road,
Which to discover we must travel too."

→ → → → → → → → → → → → →
Go on to the next page.

"That's from the *Rubáiyát* of Omar Khayyám," Miss Seymour says. "I've always loved it. The verse I like is:

I sent my Soul through the Invisible,
Some Letter of the After-life to spell:
   And by and by my Soul return'd to me,
And answer'd "I Myself am Heav'n and
      Hell."

"One of my favorites also, Miss Seymour," Lawrence says.

"Uh, thanks, but I'm not sure that answers my question," you say. "I mean, if you're good, when you die your soul goes up to heaven with the angels and God, right?"

"So some believe," Lawrence says. "But I'm beginning to feel, as those who roam the desert long enough do, that there's something in the universe that's inexpressible in words, and indeed in thought."

"That's heavy stuff," you say.

"Right you are," Lawrence says, and laughs. "Very heavy stuff."

"I'm still wondering about the things put in the tombs so the mummies can live in luxury after death," you say. "What happens when the tomb robbers take it all? I mean, according to the Egyptians?"

"I guess they then have to exist like the rest of us," Lawrence says.

If you decide to go to sleep, turn to page 24.

"I still feel sorry for them, somehow," you say. "Do you think there are any tombs that haven't been robbed?"

"Probably not. But I have a friend, an archeologist, who thinks there are. Maybe someday you'll meet him," Lawrence says.

"Aren't archeologists the ones who search for buried treasure?" you ask.

"Not really. They search for knowledge of the past. Knowledge is their reward. Sometimes they do find treasure, but it usually ends up in museums for all of us to share and enjoy," Lawrence says.

Another silence settles around the fire. You notice that the farmers have all departed silently and that the three of you are the only ones left.

"Anyone for a walk?" Lawrence says, standing up and stretching. "The moon should be up soon. It turns the desert to magic."

"It's very late," Miss Seymour says. "I should try to get some sleep."

"And *you*, how do you feel about it?" Lawrence asks.

The idea of a late-night walk in the desert sounds appealing to you. Still, you are getting tired. Perhaps you should turn in to sleep.

→ → → → → → → → → → → →

If you decide to go for a walk in the desert, turn to page 95.

← ← ← ← ← ← ← ← ← ← ← ←

If you decide to go to sleep, turn to page 24.

48

You decide not to sneak away from Miss Seymour and the guide—for the moment. Miss Seymour pushes back through the crowd and grabs you by the arm. "This place is impossible," she says, giving a scathing look to a couple of vendors who have somehow managed to follow her through the maddening crowd. They back off, finally discouraged, as Miss Seymour drags you back to the entrance of the suq. The carriage is still waiting just outside.

"I will have the driver take us back to the hotel," the guide says.

"*I'll* decide what we're doing next," Miss Seymour says. "We're going to the pyramids."

"The pyramids?" the guide says.

"That's what I said."

"But—"

"No buts about it," Miss Seymour says, pushing you into the carriage and then climbing in behind you.

The guide reluctantly, it seems, gives instructions to the driver and then climbs in also. "I'm afraid I can't take you all the way to the pyramids," he says. "But I can take you to where you can obtain camels for the last leg of your journey. Once there you will find many guides at the pyramids themselves."

"That will be fine," Miss Seymour says, settling into her seat.

← ← ← ← ← ← ← ← ← ← ← ←

Turn to page 25.

The next morning the roosters wake you up at first light. The sunrise begins as a rosy glow that fills the cloudless sky. One of the fellahin brings you a bowl of water so that you can wash your face. Another brings a pot of strong coffee and rice.

"I see that I'm just in time for breakfast," Lawrence says, suddenly appearing through the gate. He looks as fresh as if he had spent the night sleeping rather than out roaming the desert.

You finish your bowl of rice and try some of the coffee.

"Do you like the coffee?" Lawrence asks. "It's flavored with cardamom seed, an Arab specialty."

"It does taste a little strange," Miss Seymour says.

"It's very good," you say. "Really," though you've never heard of cardamom seed.

"We'll be leaving soon," Lawrence says. "I've arranged for a very special conveyance to take us to Cairo."

* * *

A short time later, you follow Lawrence out of the gate where a donkey cart is waiting. His bicycle is already in the back. A delegation of the fellahin, including some women dressed in long black robes, comes out to see you off. Lawrence climbs into the cart and helps you and Miss Seymour get aboard. Bundles of straw serve as seats. A small but sturdy-looking donkey hitched up to the cart looks back expectantly as the driver sits on a cross board in front.

"Assalaamu aleikum," Lawrence says to his friends as you start off. "Peace be with you."

"Wa aleikum assalaam," they reply. "And on you, peace."

You go back past the pyramids, resplendent and golden in the early morning light. You realize how magnificent they must have looked when their outer surfaces were finished with smooth, polished limestone, and their tops sheathed in polished gold.

The donkey cart is not the fastest way you've traveled, but in a way, it's the most fun. People on all sides wave greetings and call out *salaam* as you go past.

" *'Salaam'* means 'peace' in Arabic," Lawrence says. "It's a general greeting."

"Salaam," you repeat.

"Very good. Maybe you'll have a chance to learn some more Arabic before you leave," Lawrence says. "I think it's important to learn something of the language in whatever country you visit. Language is the key to many things."

* * *

When you arrive at the hotel, the donkey cart pulls up in front of a line of fancy carriages. This causes quite a commotion. Several uniformed porters rush out and try to shoo the cart away before they realize that two patrons of the hotel are riding in the back.

Some of the diners on the terrace get up from their meals to see what is happening. Among these are your mother and father.

"You're all right," your mother exclaims, giving you a hug. "You two had us worried."

"I trust everything is under control, Helen," your father queries.

"Yes, thanks to Mr. Lawrence here," Miss Seymour replies in an apologetic tone.

Your father recognizes T. E. Lawrence almost at once from the many descriptions he has read.

"Ah, Mr. Lawrence," your father says, coming down the front steps of the hotel.

"And you, if I may hazard a guess from the facial resemblance to young Indy here, are Professor Jones of Princeton, U.S.A."

→ → → → → → → → → → → →

Go on to the next page.

"Would you care to join us for a spot of lunch?" your father asks Lawrence, as they shake hands.

"I'd be delighted."

Together, you go up to the terrace and take seats in the wicker chairs that surround the tables. On the way, Miss Seymour fills your mother in on what happened.

"I'm so glad that I'll be able to attend your lecture this afternoon, Professor Jones," Lawrence says. "It will be the high point of my visit to Cairo. Then tomorrow I am off, up the Nile to Luxor to see an archeologist friend of mine named Howard Carter. I'm sort of baby-sitting a load of supplies for him."

"That's quite a coincidence," your father says. "We're also going up the river to Luxor. Maybe we can all go together."

"I'd love to," Lawrence says, "except . . . I'm going by dhow. They're boats designed strictly for cargo—no facilities for passengers, really."

"Maybe Indy would enjoy going that way," your father says. "His tutor could go with my wife and me on one of the more luxurious riverboats, and we'll rejoin you later."

"If Indy doesn't mind roughing it," Lawrence says.

You hate it when people talk about you as if you weren't there. You're about to say something when you realize that they're both looking at you expectantly.

This is a good chance for you to get away from Miss Seymour for a while and maybe have some fun. On the other hand, riding on a funky cargo boat as opposed to a luxurious riverboat sounds as if it leaves a lot to be desired.

← ← ← ← ← ← ← ← ← ← ← ←

If you decide to go with Lawrence up river by dhow, turn to page 35.

→ → → → → → → → → → → →

If you decide to go with your parents and Miss Seymour on the riverboat, turn to page 100.

"**I**'d better not," you say.

The boy nods, then disappears among the stones as Miss Seymour turns and comes toward you.

"I think we can dispense with a guide altogether," she says. "I gave him a piaster for his trouble—not that he was worth it. Now come along and we'll finish our climb."

Twenty minutes later, you finally reach the top. Both you and Miss Seymour are winded from the climb. Luckily you have the summit all to yourselves. You sit down and look out over the scene. To the northeast, Cairo with its gilded domes and minarets is a glistening jewel in the late afternoon light. In the west, the sun is sinking toward the wastes of the vast desert.

→ → → → → → → → → → → → →
Go on to the next page.

"The pyramid was thirty feet higher before its limestone facing was removed, mostly to provide building material for the mosques of Cairo," Miss Seymour says. "We are sitting at a spot where a capstone overlaid with polished gold crowned the pyramid. It must have mirrored the sun—at certain times of day throwing bright rays of light straight up into the sky. One theory is that the Egyptians believed that the pharaoh climbed up to heaven on those beams."

"Speaking of the sun," you say, "we'd better get down before it gets dark."

"I think you're right," Miss Seymour says with a sigh.

In many ways the climb down seems more difficult than the climb up. It's not like going down a flight of steps—you have to lower yourself off each stone one at a time. It's not that easy for Miss Seymour in her long skirt and heeled shoes.

← ← ← ← ← ← ← ← ← ← ← ←

Turn to page 39.

You sail up the river all day, past bright green strips of cultivated land on both shores, each stretching away to the gray-white desert, always off in the distance.

Here and there, small villages of mud-brick houses nestle among groves of tall palm trees. An occasional small caravan of camels appears in the distance. Closer by on the riverbank, women in long, flowing black garments fill water jugs and carry them away, gracefully balanced, on their heads. And all along the way scores of dark-skinned children splash around in the shallows near the shore. Their shouts and laughter echo across the water. Further out in the river, armadas of single-masted boats sweep past, their triangular sails curved upward like great wings.

You go upriver for another few days. At night you sleep curled up on your coil of rope, covered with a woolen blanket.

→ → → → → → → → → → → →

Go on to the next page.

"We are now about halfway to our destination," Lawrence says one afternoon. "You see that rather ordinary village over there on the east bank? It's now called Tell el Amarna, but it was once called Akhetaton, 'The Horizon of Aton.' At one time it was perhaps the greatest city in Egypt. It stretched along the Nile for over five miles. Its vanished glories hold the strangest story in Egyptian history. In many ways it's a very sad story."

"Why is that?" you ask.

"Because the city started as an ideal," Lawrence answers. "For the first time in history, the belief in one God was put forth. It ended in complete failure. Akhnaton, the 'heretic king' as the ancient Egyptians thought of him, and his elegant queen, Nefertiti, moved their capital here from Thebes.

"They built what may have been the most beautiful city in all of history. It was adorned with lavish, multicolored palaces and wide boulevards lined with flowering trees and fountains. It had untold acres of landscaped gardens. Even the poorest worker had a home with several rooms. It was known as the 'City of Flowers.'"

"What happened?" you ask.

"Trying to abolish the many gods proved to be premature," Lawrence says. "The people of Egypt didn't go for the concept. Also, the empire was crumbling while Akhnaton spent all his time worshiping his one God, Aton. The city lasted for only fifteen years."

"What happened to the king?" you ask.

"No one knows how he died. Later kings tried to erase any record or memories of him. Tutankhamen, his young son-in-law, later became king and moved the capital back to Thebes. The city of Akhetaton was then left to decay and vanish back into the desert. You know, it is believed that Tutankhamen became king somewhere around your age, and died probably around eighteen or nineteen. His tomb is one of the few that have never been discovered. My friend, Howard Carter, is determined to find it. You'll meet him soon."

The dhow continues up the Nile. You sit on your large coil of rope and try to study your textbooks. More often you stare out at the passing riverbanks, where rows of stately palms often line the shore and water buffalo wallow in the shallows. Occasionally you pass the ruins of ancient temples, some half submerged in the river.

"We'll be there early tomorrow," Lawrence says. "The ship will anchor and unload just off the west bank of the river opposite the ruins of Thebes."

"Another ancient city?"

→ → → → → → → → → → → → →

Go on to the next page.

"Yes, it was," Lawrence says. "It's too bad we can't jump back four thousand years and see it in its heyday. It had more palaces and temples than anywhere else on earth, including the largest temple ever built, the Temple of Amen-Re, the main god of Thebes. The ruins of it are still there today."

Early the next morning, you look to the west. The brilliant red-orange light of the rising sun reflects off a range of cliffs in the distance.

Lawrence comes back from the bow of the ship, his usual station, where he helps with the constant sounding—checking the depth of the water—a necessary procedure to keep the boat from running aground in the treacherous currents of the Nile.

"Those are the cliffs of Deir el-Bahri up ahead. Some of them are six hundred feet high. The Valley of the Kings, a rugged and barren area full of deep chasms, lies just on the other side of them."

"Why do they call it the Valley of the Kings?"

"That's where the later pharaohs were buried."

"It has pyramids like the one I climbed near Cairo?" you ask.

"No," Lawrence says. "The pharaohs eventually gave up on pyramids. Pyramids tended to pinpoint where the pharaohs and their treasure were buried. More than seventy pyramids were built, and all of them were later robbed. Thutmose I was the first pharaoh to hide his tomb in the desolate valley on the other side of those cliffs. The tomb chambers were cut deep into the rock and all the debris carefully carted away. After the pharaoh was buried, the site was covered over with gravel and made to look as if there was nothing there. Unfortunately, it didn't fool the tomb robbers for very long."

"How many tombs are there?" you ask.

"I'd say about fifty. They were dug over a period of five hundred years. The last tomb was being made for Rameses XI, but it was never finished, and he was never buried in it."

"That's a lot of tombs," you say. "Have they all been discovered?"

"All but a couple. But you can ask Mr. Carter about that. I think I see him over there on the riverbank waving to us."

Shouts are going from one end of the ship to the other as some sailors help to drop the anchor and others climb the masts to bring down the sails.

Two men in Western dress, surrounded by native workmen, are standing on the riverbank. One is a short and stocky man in shirtsleeves with suspenders. The other, taller but frail looking, is dressed in rumpled tweeds and sports a mustache.

→ → → → → → → → → → → →

Go on to the next page.

Behind the men is a long line of donkeys and a few horses, ready, you guess, to carry the supplies from the ship.

The workmen from the shore wade into the water up to midchest and grab bundles handed over from the ship. Lawrence shouts something, and one of the workmen pushes out a small raft made of reeds.

"Jump on that when it comes alongside, and keep your books dry," Lawrence says. He then jumps into the water and wades ashore.

When you get there yourself, Lawrence introduces you to the two men you saw from the boat standing on shore, Howard Carter and Lord Carnarvon.

"Good to have you with us," Carter tells you. "Do you prefer to ride a horse or a donkey?"

Your father taught you to ride at a stable not far from Princeton last year. "A horse," you say, welcoming the opportunity to ride once again.

The horse turns out to be small and gentle. You trot along behind Carter, Lord Carnarvon, and Lawrence, also riding horses. You follow along on a narrow, sandy path, making your way through green fields and past groves of palm trees. Suddenly you come to the edge of the desert where the road becomes wider and lined with pebbles. A great, flat, barren plain stretches ahead of you, leading up all the way to the cliffs in the far distance.

→ → → → → → → → → → → →

Go on to the next page.

Carter's camp is basically a double row of tents near the base of the towering cliffs. When you get there, Carter and Lord Carnarvon dismount and immediately go off to the bottom of the cliffs where the tomb they are excavating is located. Lawrence takes you over and introduces you to the foreman.

"This my good friend, Rashid Sallam," he says to you.

You shake hands with Rashid who, as he takes your hand, is suddenly distracted. A short distance away, a group of workmen sit in a circle. A short, bald, and overweight Arabic man is talking to them.

"Mr. Ghaly!" Rashid calls over. "May I have a word with you?"

The man comes over, moving somewhat reluctantly.

"Why are the men back here in camp, and idle?" Rashid asks.

"They are afraid."

"Afraid? Afraid of what?"

"They say there is a curse on the tomb. Anyone who enters will die soon after."

"Ridiculous!" Rashid says. "You know there is no such thing as a curse."

"But that is what they are saying."

"Tell them to get back to the excavation at once!"

Go on to the next page.

Mr. Ghaly goes back, looking like he's wading in quicksand.

"I don't trust that man," Rashid explains. "He's been told many times not to allow the use of dynamite to clear the roads close to the excavations. But he does it anyway. In addition, he's a poor overseer. I must talk to Carter about him."

"But there *could* be a curse, couldn't there?" you ask.

"Absolutely not. It's pure superstition!" Rashid says.

You look over and see Carter and Lord Carnarvon coming back into camp. They are carrying a wooden box and seem very excited.

"One of the workmen found these small clay shards at the base of the cliffs. Rashid, make sure the workman gets a reward. His name is Habib," Carter says.

"I'll see to it," Rashid says.

"The amazing thing here is this small cartouche stamped into this piece," Carter says. He excitedly takes the shard out of the box. "It's the seal of Tutankhamen."

A gasp goes up from several of those listening.

"Tutankhamen!" Rashid says. "Then you know what this means."

→ → → → → → → → → → → →

Go on to the next page.

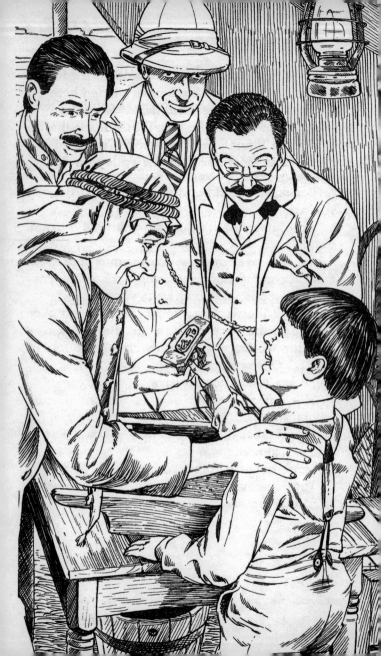

"Now, let's not jump to conclusions," Carter says. "The pieces could have been carried here from anywhere. I've been told that a secret tunnel exists somewhere near here that leads to the Valley of the Kings. The location of Tutankhamen's tomb is most likely in the valley on the other side."

"Is that the Tut . . . Tutankhamen you were telling me about on the river?" you ask Lawrence.

"That's right," Lawrence says.

"Here, take a look," Carter says, handing you the shard. "You see the small seal here. The outside shape—round at the top and bottom, and resting on a short, horizontal line at the bottom—indicates that it's a royal name. The bird, a quail, and the two half-rounds spell TUT. The cross shape with the loop on top is ANKH, the symbol of life. The three elements at the top spell AMEN, God of Thebes. There you have it—TUTANKHAMEN."

"That's like an actual alphabet," you say. "I always thought they were just little pictures."

→ → → → → → → → → → → → →

Go on to the next page.

"Some of the hieroglyphs are, but very few are used as actual pictures," Carter tells you. "The *ankh* you see here, originally a sandal strap, stands for life and was popularly used on charms. Only about twenty-four hieroglyphs were used as the alphabet as we know it. Most stood for combinations of two or three sounds."

"I'd like to learn more about them," you say.

"You will," Carter says.

"Do you still plan to open the second chamber in the tomb today?" Rashid asks Carter.

"Certainly."

"Have you determined whose tomb it is?" Lawrence asks.

"From the inscriptions inside, it seems to be a rather modest royal tomb of the eighteenth dynasty, but certainly not of a pharaoh. The person's name was Amenhotep, which means 'Amen is Satisfied'—a popular name for minor royalty in that dynasty."

"Do you still want me to scout out the Valley of the Kings?" Rashid asks. "We still don't have permission to dig there."

"We will have it one of these days," Carter says expectantly. Then he turns to you. "Perhaps our young friend here might want to go along with you," he says to Rashid.

"How about it?" Rashid asks you. "We can ride our horses out there and take a look."

You take a moment to think. You would like to see the Valley of the Kings, but you would also like to stick around and see the opening of the second chamber in the tomb.

→　→　→　→　→　→　→　→　→　→　→　→

If you decide to go with Rashid to the Valley of the Kings, turn to page 107.

←　←　←　←　←　←　←　←　←　←　←　←

If you decide to stay and see the opening of the tomb, turn to page 13.

"**D**ad! Mom! Miss Seymour!" you call out. But they don't hear you over the noise of the crowd. You push your way through and catch up with them.

"A thief stole my book bag, and—" you start.

"I'm sorry," your father says. "But we won't be able to find anyone in this mob of people. You'll just have to do without it."

Two carriages are waiting for you at the foot of the dock, one to carry you, your parents, and Miss Seymour—the other to carry your luggage, which is already being unloaded from the ship. The carriage takes you to a train station not far away. There you board a railroad car elaborately decorated with mahogany paneling and broad seats upholstered in finely woven fabrics.

"This is some fancy car!" you say.

"Yes," your father says. "Usually it's reserved for British officers and their families. The Egyptians, if they can afford to travel by train at all, are confined to the boxcars. You're getting your first taste of British imperialism."

You sit on one of the plush seats by the window. "Is Cairo far away?" you ask.

"About a hundred and thirty-five miles," your father says. "We'll be there in a few hours."

← ← ← ← ← ← ← ← ← ← ← ←
Turn to page 17.

"After you die," Carter says, "you make your way through the dark caverns of the underworld until you meet the 'Questioner.' He asks, 'What is your name?' After telling him your name, you continue through the underworld until you get to the jury of the gods, who will then decide if you deserve permanent death or immortal life."

"Like judgment day in the Christian religion?" you ask.

"Somewhat similar," Carter says. "You see, here is Osiris, chief god of the underworld, and beside him is Anubis, the jackal-headed god of burial. Now over here, you approach the scales guarded by both the sun god, Horus, and Maat, the goddess of truth. They lay your heart on one side of the scales, and put a feather on the other side. If your heart is heavier than the feather, you are immediately devoured by Amemit, the 'eater of souls,' a monster with the head of a crocodile."

You feel a bit faint. "Doesn't seem to give you much of a chance. I mean weighing your heart against a feather," you say.

"I wouldn't worry too much about it," Lawrence says with a wink. "No one really knows what happens to you after death, now do they?"

"I think we're ready to open the inner door," Carter says.

→ → → → → → → → → → → →
Go on to the next page.

"Hold on a minute," Lord Carnarvon says. "What do you make of this inscription over the door? I can almost read it, but a few of the words escape me."

"Let me see," Carter says. He scans it for a few seconds. "Ah, yes. I have it: 'Death will come on swift wings to any who defiles this tomb.'"

"Then there *is* a curse!" you say.

"These inscriptions are quite common," Carter says. "Of the many dozens of people, including myself, who have gone into tombs, I don't know of any to whom death has come 'on swift wings.'"

"Still . . ." you say.

"Are you afraid?" Lawrence asks you.

"Who, me?" you say. "Of course not. Let's see what's in there."

"Good for you," Carter says. "Now stand back while I pry open this door with a crowbar."

Suddenly there is a hissing sound, like escaping air. Green smoke starts seeping out of the sides of the door.

"Everyone out, quickly!" Carter shouts.

You run out, your heart pounding. Carter comes out last, coughing a bit. "We got out just in time," he says. "But it was close."

"What is it? Poison gas?" Lord Carnarvon asks.

"I'm not sure. But the tomb robbers probably released most of it long ago. Otherwise we'd not be talking to one another now," Carter says. "In any event, I pried open the door all the way at the last moment. We'll let it air out for a while, then go back inside and take another look."

You wait outside for an hour or so. Carter is impatient to get back in. Finally, no longer able to wait, he goes cautiously back down into the tomb. A short time later, he calls up from the entrance. "The gas seems to have dissipated."

You, Lawrence, and Lord Carnarvon follow him inside. In the center of the second room is a large sarcophagus, but otherwise the room is empty. The sarcophagus is covered with a stone lid.

"Shall we see what's inside?" Carter says, as the four of you gather around it. "When I count to three, we'll all push. Ready, one, two, three—push!"

Together you all strain. The lid shifts slowly with a grating sound, sliding down toward the bottom end. The top part of the sarcophagus is now open. Everyone looks in.

"My God!" Lawrence exclaims.

→ → → → → → → → → → → → →

Go on to the next page.

"Is that Amenhotep?" Lord Carnarvon asks.

"It is," Carter says.

"Holy-smokes," you say.

The mummy's upper half is unwrapped. From the waist down, as far as you can see, it is swathed in layers of blackened strips of cloth. The skull, with shrunken dried skin still stretched tightly over it, grins up at you eerily. The exposed part of the torso is also shrunken and cracked, and the arms are folded over the chest, with the long boney fingers curled inward.

"Extraordinary!" Carter says.

"There's no jewelry or other artifacts," Lord Carnarvon says.

"I guess those were stolen long ago when robbers rifled the tomb," Carter says. "There may still be some hidden in the lower wrappings, but we'll have to wait until later when we can carefully unwrap the mummy."

You stand there, horrified and yet fascinated by the mummy, reflecting on your lessons and all you that have just learned.

Then you hear a familiar voice from outside the tomb calling your name. You recognize it as Miss Seymour's.

"It's time for you to start back home. Your parents are waiting for you," she says when you go back out.

→ → → → → → → → → → → →

Go on to the next page.

"I guess this is farewell for the moment," Lawrence says.

"I'll write to you," you say.

"Maybe you'll write to me in hieroglyphs," he says.

"Maybe," you say.

You say good-bye to Mr. Carter and Lord Carnarvon, then start back toward the Nile. Your long trip home is just beginning, and so is your life of travel and adventure.

The End

You decide to sneak away from Miss Seymour for a while. Backing out of the crowd, you quickly look around. There are many side streets, narrow overhung alleyways leading from the main area of the market. It takes you only a few seconds to pick one out.

The narrow street is crowded with shops on both sides. Every kind of merchandise imaginable spills out into the street itself. You figure you'll explore for a few blocks, then head back and find Miss Seymour.

You come across a lot of jewelers. They sit cross-legged in front of their tiny shops, fashioning small, delicate pieces of jewelry in gold and silver. Each block seems more fascinating than the last. As you walk, you get drawn deeper and deeper into the maze of narrow alleyways.

You turn to the left down one street, then to the right down another as different shops catch your eye. Suddenly you realize that you should be getting back to Miss Seymour. You try to retrace your steps, but the more you try, the more confused you become.

You pass a shop filled with large, embroidered cushions. You passed that once before, you remember. You must be going around in circles. Just try going in a straight line and you'll come out somewhere, you tell yourself.

→ → → → → → → → → → → → →

Go on to the next page.

However, it's not that easy, it turns out. The streets twist and turn, throwing you off. Still, you try and do your best to keep going in one direction.

Soon you leave the shops behind, and the streets become quiet, almost deserted. You're starting to get scared.

Then, up ahead, you see a large, open gateway with a garden inside. When you get there, you stop to look. In the center, water is flowing down a marble fountain with a bubbling sound. There is no one around.

"Hello!" you call out. But there is no answer.

On the other side of the garden is a stairway that leads to an apartment above. Maybe you can find someone there who can give you directions back to the market.

You go up the stairway to a balcony overlooking the garden, and then over to the open doorway of the apartment. Inside, the floors are covered with richly patterned carpets. The large windows way on the other side of the room have wooden screens perforated with interwoven geometric patterns. The sunlight from outside gently filters through them.

There is almost no furniture in the room, but a man dressed in a dark blue robe and a white turban is sitting cross-legged in front of a small, richly decorated octagonal table. His back is to you, but you can see that he is reading a book.

You knock gently on the door frame.

→ → → → → → → → → → → →

Go on to the next page.

The man turns to face in your direction, then gracefully gets to his feet. *"Salaam aleikum,"* he says, cupping his hands and bowing slightly. *"Afwan ya akhi."*

You guess that this means "hello" in his language. "I'm sorry," you say. "I only speak English."

"Ah, you are English, my friend. I should have guessed. My name is Gamal Mahmed. And what brings you to my humble home?"

"Actually, I'm American," you say. "I got lost in the market and ended up here."

"You have wandered far, my friend. I will see to it that you return safely."

Just then, from somewhere outside, you hear a strange cry—a cross between a song and a wail.

"You must excuse me, my friend. That is the muezzin. It's call means that it is time for me to pray. I will only be a few moments. If you wish, you may sit by the table and look at this," he says, handing you the book he was reading.

"Thanks," you say.

Gamal kneels on the floor and taps his forehead to the carpet several times, reciting softly something in Arabic.

Meanwhile, you look through the book. The Arabic writing looks like some kind of shorthand gone crazy, but the illustrations, miniature paintings of people, gardens, and trees, are beautiful.

"Thank you," Gamal says, coming over to the table. "The muezzin calls believers to prayer five times a day: daybreak, noon, midafternoon, sunset, and after nightfall. Each time, we faithful must face toward Mecca and pray. The sacred book you are holding is the Koran."

"That's like our Bible," you say.

"Much like it. Many of the people in it are the same. Abraham, Moses, and Jesus are all highly praised in the Koran."

"Then you worship Allah the same way we worship God, right?"

"Allah is our name for God, just as God is your name for God."

"That's confusing," you say.

"Maybe we all worship the same God and don't realize it," Gamal says.

"What does this say right here?" you ask, pointing to the lower part of a page in the book. "I like the picture above the writing."

"Let me see. Oh, yes. It says . . . 'After death the righteous will be transported to Paradise and recline on jeweled couches in eternal shade, amidst gushing water and abundant fruits. Those who reject Allah will dwell among scorching winds and boiling waters.'"

"Like heaven and hell," you say.

→ → → → → → → → → → → →

Go on to the next page.

"Yes," Gamal says. "But the words of the sacred Koran are very difficult to translate into English or any other language. Their poetry is lost. If you could read Arabic, you would understand. Perhaps if we had more time. But right now, I must take you back to the market."

You follow Gamal out of his house and through the streets. He seems well-known. Many people greet him by name as he goes by.

When you reach the market, you can't find Miss Seymour or the guide. "Can you tell me how to get back to my hotel?" you ask Gamal, telling him the name.

"I will take you there," he says.

Gamal seems to know a lot of shortcuts through the city, and soon you reach the hotel.

"I will leave you here at the entrance," Gamal says. "So *haz saiid,* or 'good luck' as you say in English."

"You must come in and meet my mother and father," you say. "It would help if you explained to my tutor, Miss Seymour, that I got lost."

"I'm afraid it would be embarrassing for your parents if I did so. As strange as it may seem, we Egyptians are not welcome in this hotel, even though it is in our own country."

At that moment a carriage pulls up. Your father and Miss Seymour get out. She lets out a small cry when she sees you. Then she looks as if she's about to give you a rap on the ear.

→   →   →   →   →   →   →   →   →   →   →   →

Go on to the next page.

"It's all right, Helen," your father says. "Indy here seems safe and sound."

"This is Gamal Mahmed," you say. "He helped me find my way back."

"There's a scholar of Arab medieval history by that name," your father says.

"I must humbly confess that I am that person," Gamal says.

"I'm a student of medieval history myself," your father says. "As such, I am eternally grateful to the Arabs for preserving our classical heritage during the Dark Ages of Europe. I'm also beholden to you for young Indy's safety. Come, I must treat you to lunch."

"I don't think—" Gamal starts.

"I insist on it, come," your father says.

Your mother joins the rest of you on the terrace. There are a few dirty looks from the other patrons because of Gamal, but Gamal couldn't seem to care less. He and your father get into a discussion about history that leaves you far behind. Instead you concentrate on the luncheon.

Finally, your father turns to you and says, "You should start to get packed. Tomorrow we're going to start on a four-hundred-mile trip up the Nile to the ruins of Karnak."

You bid Gamal farewell, and once again thank him for seeing you back safely. You say goodnight to your parents and to Miss Seymour, then head back to your room and pack.

→ → → → → → → → → → → → →

Turn to page 101.

It may be a long time before you visit the pyramids again, so you decide to take the boy up on his offer and go and see the secret passage.

He leads you away from the crowd and along a narrow ledge of stones high up on the pyramid.

"In here," he says, vanishing among the stones on the side. You follow close behind and find the narrow opening he squeezed through. The first several feet are tight, but then the tunnel widens. The boy picks up a small kerosene lamp from the floor and lights it with a three-inch-long match. You see that the floor is smooth but that the walls and ceiling are of ragged stone.

You introduce yourself.

"My name is Ramses," the boy says.

"Wasn't there a pharaoh named Ramses?" you ask.

"Many pharaohs. The name has been in my family for thousands of years."

"Is that your real name?" you ask suspiciously.

"It is, truly," he says, starting off down the tunnel. You follow him. "And we are also Christians. Coptic Christians."

"Really?" you say, and think for a moment. "Wait a minute, now I know you're kidding."

→ → → → → → → → → → → →

Go on to the next page.

"Most of the people you see in our country are Arabs, but there are still many of us Coptic Christians around," Ramses says. "We are like the Indians in America. Before the Arabs invaded and took over our country, all the people here were like us. But the Arabs slowly wiped most of us out. 'Copts,' as we are called, means 'people of Egypt.' We are the true Egyptians. The others are invaders. Our Coptic language is the same as the ancients, though we've been forced to also learn the Arabic language of our conquerors in order to survive."

"You also speak very good English," you say.

"That is also to survive," Ramses says. "I learn much from tourists like you."

"I guess I am a tourist," you say. You've been traveling for so long, you were starting to feel more like a native.

"That's all right. Tourists are very good." Ramses turns into a side passage leading slightly upward, then goes into another one.

"Where are we going? And what is this tunnel?" you ask. "You said that no one else knows about it. Is that really true?"

Ramses laughs. "There are many tunnels through the pyramid. Only I know them all. The plans for the inside of the pyramid were changed several times during the building. Many tunnels were left as they were when they made new ones. Tunnels were made for the workmen to get air and to escape when the ceremonial tunnels were sealed with tons of stone. They never filled in the tunnels of the workmen."

"That was dumb," you say. "The tomb robbers could use them to get to the pharaoh's treasure and—"

"They would never find their way out. These tunnels are like a maze. You want to try? Look behind you."

You turn to see what Ramses is pointing at. "I don't see—" you start. When you turn back, he is gone, but the lantern is on the stone floor in front of you.

"Ramses, come back!" you shout. The sound of your voice echoes through the tunnels.

He must be playing games, you realize. Well I'll show him, you say to yourself. It can't be that hard to find your way back. You can remember how many turns you made in the tunnels.

→ → → → → → → → → → → → →
Go on to the next page.

This was a right turn, you think. Farther on, it was a left turn, you're sure. But the way you're going doesn't seem to lead to the outside. You go back and try a different way. This leads to a dead end—a blank wall with crude, ancient Egyptian symbols roughly scratched on the stone. They had graffiti even back then, you realize.

You go back and try another way. Still no luck.

"Okay, Ramses, I give up. Do you hear me?"

But there is nothing but silence.

You sit there for a while on the floor, your back up against the rough stone wall. It's not very comfortable. What a fix, trapped inside the Great Pyramid. Ramses is right, robbers wouldn't be able to find their way out of here.

The lamp flickers, getting low on oil. Then, a strong draft blows through the tunnel, almost blowing the flame out.

"You did very well," Ramses says, appearing out of the darkness. "You made only a couple of wrong turns, otherwise you might have found your way to the surface. But you would have never have found the treasure."

"Treasure?" you say. "You mean there's still treasure in here?"

"I cannot say. I have been sworn to silence by the ancients."

"Come on, Ramses, no more games."

→ → → → → → → → → → → →

Go on to the next page.

"I will tell you a secret then. I am really a pharaoh."

"Sure you are, Ramses."

Ramses takes hold of your arm. "No, I tell you the truth. I am a descendant of the ancient kings. My parents told me so."

"All right then, when you die will you be made into a mummy and have a tomb for all your riches?"

"I will. It is being built for me right now in the City of the Dead near the Citadel. It will be a grand house of stone with my burial vault beneath it. There will be a courtyard where my relatives can bring food and other things for me."

"But you said you were a Christian."

"I am."

"Then how can you believe that—"

"No more questions or I will vanish again."

"No, not that. I have to get back to my tutor."

"All right, then, follow me," Ramses says mysteriously.

Soon you see light from the outside streaming down the narrow corridor. "Thanks for showing me the secret passage. I know you think you had me scared, but I wasn't really," you say, not completely telling the truth.

Suddenly, Ramses disappears from in front of you. You know that he probably just ducked into some niche on the side of the passageway, but it's still very strange. You wonder if he really is a pharaoh. Perhaps you just imagined this whole episode.

When you get outside, it's almost dark. Miss Seymour is sitting on a stone just outside the main tourist entrance to the inside of the pyramid. It's now deserted. She looks mad as a hornet.

"There you are!" she says angrily. "I saw you walk away and disappear up the side of the pyramid. Where were you?"

"I went inside the pyramid through a secret tunnel. I met a pharaoh."

"I think the pyramid has affected your senses, that's what I think," Miss Seymour berates you. "I don't want to hear another word about it. I'm mad enough already. Just start down the pyramid and don't wander out of my sight again."

You have no choice but to do as you're told.

← ← ← ← ← ← ← ← ← ← ← ← ←
Turn to page 39.

"I'll go with you," you tell Lawrence. "If you're sure it isn't too dangerous—I mean bandits and all that."

"No, it isn't dangerous," Lawrence reassures you. "We will be shadows in the night, roaming the desert with the hyenas and the wild dogs."

"Won't they attack us?"

"Not if you're with me," Lawrence says. "I know their language. Many a night I've gone out and howled at the moon with them."

"I don't have to howl, do I?" you ask.

"Not unless you feel like it. Anyway, silence is best. Are you ready?"

"Sure," you say, getting to your feet.

Miss Seymour also gets to her feet. "I'm going with you," she says. "I'm not going to lie awake all night worrying about Indy wandering around out there in the desert."

"Good show!" Lawrence says. "But hold on a moment." He goes into the house and comes back with several hooded robes. "We'll carry these for a while. We may need to wear them later on."

The three of you go out through the gate and into the night. A full moon is rising on the eastern horizon. It hangs brilliant and enormous over Cairo.

"I've never seen a moon that big," you say.

In the moonlight, the pyramids are bright, almost as if they were lit by floodlights.

→ → → → → → → → → → → →

Go on to the next page.

"Can you imagine how they must have looked when their limestone outer casings were smoothed and polished into seamless sheets?" Miss Seymour asks.

"Perhaps more spectacular in moonlight than in sunlight," Lawrence says.

You walk past the Sphinx, also illuminated and mysterious.

"They say that the Sphinx, that human-headed lion, was once coated with plaster and painted to look lifelike—ready to pounce on anyone daring to desecrate the sacred precincts surrounding the pyramids," Lawrence says.

"Lifelike?" you say, getting a little spooked.

"We'll just tiptoe past and hope that it doesn't notice us," Lawrence says.

You follow a road past the pyramids until nothing but the vast desert lies before you. The moon is higher, and your long shadows reach out like fingers toward the west.

You keep walking. Strangely, none of you feels like talking for a while. Lawrence was right, you realize; there's something out here in the desert you can't put into words. You walk as if in a trance—almost hypnotized by the weird beauty and strangeness.

"Do you think we could stop and sit down for a bit?" Miss Seymour says, finally. "My legs are about to give out."

"I'm sorry, I didn't realize . . ." Lawrence says.

"Once I get started, I can walk forever in the desert. Come, over here would be a good place."

Lawrence walks to the side of a sand dune just off the road, then lies down on his back with his hands behind his head, looking up at the sky. The moon is now almost overhead. The distant pyramids are small, silver triangles on the horizon behind you.

"I could live in the desert all my life," Lawrence says, "wandering with the beduins, a life free of material attachments. No worries, only the sky above and the sand below."

"I think you might be wasting your life, then," Miss Seymour says. "I have a feeling that you have great things to accomplish. As does young Indy here." She turns to you. "That is, when you realize how important your studies are."

"I guess I agree in a way," Lawrence says. "But in the end what does it all mean? Fame and fortune? Maybe better, as the *Rubáiyát* says, to just enjoy the moment and let the future take care of itself."

"Nothing was ever accomplished by—" Miss Seymour starts, then stops and sits upright, looking off into the distance.

"What is that?" she says, pointing to the west.

A line of moving shapes is headed in your direction.

"Ah, listen carefully, and you shall have your answer."

→ → → → → → → → → → → → →

Go on to the next page.

You are quiet. A faint jingling comes from across the sand.

"Camel bells," Lawrence says. "A caravan is coming our way."

Soon the shapes grow larger as the camels come clopping up the road. The camels are loaded with bundles and their drivers walk beside them. But the procession also includes a few unloaded donkeys, probably meant for sale in Cairo.

When the caravan arrives, Lawrence goes out to meet it. He talks to the chief driver in Arabic, then comes back over to you and Miss Seymour. "I've arranged for you to ride back to the farmhouse on two of their donkeys. I'm going to go a bit farther on, but I'll be back in the morning."

You are about to protest that you can keep going on foot when you realize how tired your legs really are. The driver helps you and Miss Seymour to mount the donkeys. Then you wave good-bye to Lawrence as the caravan starts off again.

← ← ← ← ← ← ← ← ← ← ←
Turn to page 49.

You decide to go with your parents and Miss Seymour on the riverboat.

"Thanks for the offer, though. I hope we meet again someday," you tell Lawrence.

"I have a feeling that we will. Until then, write if you have the chance. Every so often, I pick up my mail in England."

"I will," you say.

Lawrence and your father shake hands.

"I'm looking forward to your lecture," Lawrence says. "And thank you again for lunch."

Lawrence bids farewell to your mother and Miss Seymour. You watch as he then goes back to the donkey cart, now parked on the other side of the street. He pulls out his bicycle and pedals away. You hope you will see him again someday.

→ → → → → → → → → → → → →

Go on to the next page.

Early the following morning you are ready for your trip upriver. Your family's luggage is loaded in the back of a carriage, and then you, your parents, and Miss Seymour get inside.

There is a festive air at the dock when you arrive at the riverboat. The send-off is like a giant social picnic, with the guests from the hotel dressed in their finest. Even those who are not leaving on the boat have come down to see their friends and family off.

As you board the gleaming white steamer, you are amazed, trying to take it all in. More than a block long, the boat has huge paddle wheels amidships and upper and lower decks.

"Your mother and I have a stateroom on the upper deck," your father says. "You and Helen each have your own cabin directly below us."

You groan. A cabin next to Miss Seymour's— you know what that means. It looks like it's back to the books for you.

You see a number of kids, several your age, getting on the boat. That's a hopeful sign. Maybe you can make some friends on the trip—that is, if Miss Seymour ever lets you out of your cabin and away from your books long enough.

As the boat drifts away from the shore, everyone on board and on the dock waves hysterically. You stand on the railing, watching the city retreating as the boat steams southward.

An hour goes by. You are now sitting comfortably in a wicker chair on the starboard deck. So far, you haven't looked at a book, just the sky overhead and the passing riverbank.

Suddenly Miss Seymour appears. "I'm glad you're on this side of the ship," she says. "There's something important for you to see. There it is, way over there across the desert. Do you see it?"

"I think so," you say. "It's some kind of pyramid, but there are steps."

"That's right, six giant steps to be exact. It's the very first pyramid, and the world's oldest, large-scale stone structure. It was built about 2700 B.C. for King Zoser of the third dynasty by Imhotep, his brilliant architect. Imhotep was one of the great geniuses of all time. He is said to be the father of medicine. He said that disease was caused by 'worms' so tiny that they couldn't be seen. Now we call them germs, but that was four and a half thousand years ago. A bit ahead of his time, wouldn't you say?"

→ → → → → → → → → → → → →
Go on to the next page.

"He sounds like a great man," you say.

"In his lifetime, Imhotep took Egyptian architecture from mud brick construction to large-scale buildings made of finely cut stone," Miss Seymour says. "But anyway, that's enough for now. I just didn't want you to miss it. I think you've had enough studying for the time being. It's time you relaxed and enjoyed your vacation."

"Really?" you say.

"Yes, really," Miss Seymour says. "I know you think of me as a stern taskmaster, but . . . well, we can go into it some other time."

Miss Seymour goes off, and for most of the journey upriver you don't see much of her. From time to time when you do see her, she is laughing and joking with some of the other passengers. You guess she has finally decided to take a vacation herself.

It's funny—in a way you actually begin missing your studies. Sometimes you go into your cabin and read on your own. That is, when you're not talking to Amanda, a girl you have met on the boat. She's English, your own age, and she happens to have the seat next to yours at dinner. Her mother is a librarian at Oxford. Unfortunately, all she seems to be interested in is reading sappy novels by Thomas Hardy. Instead, you try to get her interested in Egyptology.

"Do you know about the opening of the mouth ceremony of the mummy?" you ask her at dinner.

"No, but it sounds simply dreadful."

"Well, the priest," you go on, undeterred, "representing the jackal-headed god of death, Anubis, restores the vital functions to the mummy by opening the eyes and mouth with special instruments."

"Do we have to talk about this at dinner?" she asks.

"I guess not," you say with a sigh. "How about later, on deck?"

"Indiana Jones, I think you are very strange," she says.

When you do see her later, she immediately goes into a discussion of the unfairness of life as depicted in *Tess of the d'Urbervilles*. You try to think of something to add to the conversation, but somehow you can't relate to what she's saying. A few times you do seem to get her interested in ancient Egypt, like the time you tell her that the mummies were buried piled up with beautiful flowers and that certain of these still show some color thousands of years later. It's not Thomas Hardy, but at least you have her interest.

After two weeks of traveling on the river, the boat finally arrives at Luxor, not far from the famous ruins at Karnak.

"Thank you for all the wonderful things you told me about mummies," Amanda says, shaking your hand good-bye.

→ → → → → → → → → → → → →
Go on to the next page.

You thank Amanda for sharing her novel with you, but you don't really mean it. However, as you say good-bye, you wonder if you'll ever get to see her again.

You and your family check into a hotel, and the next day the four of you take a carriage ride out to the ruins of ancient Luxor and the temple of Amen-Re. As you look around, you feel as if you are wandering in an endless forest of unbelievably huge pillars. They make you feel dwarfed, almost as if you're on another planet.

A few days later, you take another boat back to Cairo. There an ocean liner takes you back to the States and regular school.

Your opinion of Miss Seymour certainly changed on the trip. You gradually realized what a human and sympathetic person she really is under her "official" exterior.

School is also never quite the same, since you've actually been to many of the places you're studying about.

You do, however, get restless just sitting behind your desk at school. There are so many exciting places in the world to visit, and so many adventures out there just waiting for you. But for now they'll just have to wait. Your lifetime of adventure has only just begun. In time you will get to see *all* the wonders you dream about.

The End

You and Rashid ride horseback over the barren plains toward the entrance to the Valley of the Kings. Off in the distance, up against the base of the cliffs, are a number of temple ruins.

"Those were mortuary temples," Rashid says. "The ancient Egyptians built them farther away from the actual locations of their hidden tombs as an added protection."

Soon you come to a wide gap through the cliffs. Barren hills rise on both sides of the road.

"Do you like working for Mr. Carter?" you ask.

"Very much," Rashid says. "He treats me like an equal."

"Have you ever found any buried treasure?"

Rashid laughs. "People always ask about treasure. Treasure has a different meaning for archeologists. Each artifact they find is not valuable for them in the way that most people think. For the archeologist these artifacts are priceless because of what they tell about ancient peoples."

"Like the buried treasure of Tutankhamen?"

"Yes, if it exists. Mr. Carter is about the only one who believes that it does. Virtually all other archeologists believe that all the tombs in the valley have been found."

"What do you think?"

"I think that if anyone is going to find Tutankhamen's tomb, it will be Mr. Carter. He has kept careful records of every discovery in the valley, no matter how insignificant."

→ → → → → → → → → → → → →

Go on to the next page.

"And he has drawn up a map, I've seen it," Rashid continues enthusiastically. "It divides the valley into workable squares. He intends, when he gets permission from the government, to examine every square on the ground, no matter how long it takes him. Lord Carnarvon, his patron, will back him financially to the very end."

You come to a bluff overlooking the Valley of the Kings itself. Far below, you see several rectangular openings in the ground where tombs are being excavated.

"Tutankhamen may be hidden down there somewhere," Rashid says. "I hope, for Mr. Carter's sake, he is."

"It could be anywhere," you say, looking around.

Rashid takes out a small notebook and makes some sketches. Then the two of you sit there on your horses, looking down for a long time. You try to visualize the long and colorful procession from Thebes across the river—the attendants of the pharaoh carrying all his possessions to bury them underground. It's hard to imagine it, though, in such a desolate place.

You and Rashid turn your horses back toward Carter's camp. It's time for you to start heading back. If Tutankhamen is out there, his discovery will have to wait for another day.

The End

You decide to try and catch the boy that stole your book bag. "Stop! Thief! He's stolen my bag!" you cry out as you push through the crowd in the direction that the boy has disappeared. But soon you begin to think there are just too many people on the pier for you to be able to find him.

You are about to give up and go back when you catch sight of the boy at the far end of the pier up ahead. He is still clutching your book bag. He turns and sees you coming after him.

I've got him now, you think. But just as you close in, he dashes up the ramp to the cargo door at the stern of the ship tied up at the dock. You run after him—right into the hold.

Inside, it's piled up with huge bales of cotton as tall as you are. There are a few narrow spaces in between, and even though there's bright sunlight outside, the light here is murky, with dark shadows in the depths of the cavernous space.

A longshoreman calls out to you in Arabic as you start to squeeze between the bales. You are about to stop and go over to him when you see a slight movement among the bales. It's the thief!

Your only chance to catch him, you reason, is to get on top of the bales and look down into the spaces in between. You climb up the side of one of them, then go along, jumping from the top of one to another.

→ → → → → → → → → → → →

Go on to the next page.

Just then you see the boy, dashing back toward the door of the cargo hold. You switch direction too suddenly, and you lose your balance. You topple off one of the bales—headfirst. Your head hits something very hard, then everything goes black.

When you come to, you're in almost total darkness. Your head is throbbing from the blow it took when you hit the deck.

The churning of the ship's engine vibrates from somewhere below the floor. The whole ship is gently rocking back and forth. Oh, no—you've set sail again! You get up and feel along through the spaces between the bales. Finally you see a dim, rectangular strip of light up ahead, outlining a closed door.

You feel around for a handle and open the door. On the other side is a metal catwalk, suspended high above the engine room. Down below, a line of laborers, stripped to the waist, shovels coal into the gaping red mouths of the furnaces that fire the ship. Waves of heat hit you as you cross the walkway to a door on the other side.

The next door, you are relieved to find, opens into a short corridor with a metal stairway going up. At the top is another corridor, a wide one, lined with wood paneling and doors on both sides.

As you start down the corridor, a ship's officer comes out of one of the doors. You recognize him from your trip over—he's the chief engineer. He stops and looks at you, startled.

"My word!" he exclaims. "You're *still* aboard? How did that happen?"

"It's sort of hard to explain," you start. "You see this thief—"

"I think you'd better explain it to the captain," he says.

He leads you up another flight of stairs. They lead to the bridge, where the captain stands, steering and commanding the ship. He, too, is startled to see you, but you quickly explain what happened.

"I must say, I admire your courage in going after that dastardly thief, but we've arrived at a most difficult situation here. We're at sea, well away from land at the moment. Your parents must be worried sick."

"Isn't there some way I can get off the ship and go back?" you ask.

"Quite impossible," the captain says. "You'll have to stay with us until we reach Port Said and the Suez Canal."

"Isn't there anything—" you start.

"Wait! I have an idea," he says, beckoning for you to follow.

→ → → → → → → → → → → → →

Go on to the next page.

Together you go to a small room near the bridge, stacked up with electrical equipment.

"This is a new device I had installed just before we left England," the captain says. "It's called a 'wireless telegraph.' It can actually send messages through the air over long distances. I know that sounds quite impossible. I thought so myself at first. But I've already sent one message from sea, and got a reply."

The captain writes a short message on a pad of paper and gives it to the operator seated at a small table with a telegraph key.

The message reads: *Henry Jones, Junior, safe at sea on the* Dorchester, *on way to Port Said. Please inform parents in Alexandria.*

The operator scans the message and starts tapping the key. *Dit dit dah dah dit . . .*

"That's International Morse Code," the captain says. "It's a system of dots and dashes. For example 'S' is three dots—*dit dit dit*—and 'O' is three dashes—*dah dah dah.* If we were in trouble at sea, sinking for example, we would send *dit dit dit, dah dah dah, dit dit dit,* standing for 'SOS,' or 'Save Our Souls,' the international distress signal."

The operator finishes sending the message, then looks up. "Message sent, sir," he says. "We'll have to wait and see now if we get a confirmation."

→ → → → → → → → → → →

Go on to the next page.

Just then the companion key starts clicking again, this time without anyone touching it, as if operated by an invisible hand.

"That's it, sir!" the operator exclaims. "They're acknowledging our message."

"Remarkable," the captain says. "I think everything will work out all right after all."

Everything does work out all right, *sort* of. The captain receives a wireless message—instructions from your parents to take you to the port of Suez at the other end of the canal. From there you can take a camel caravan across the desert to Cairo.

A month later, when you finally arrive in Cairo, you're just in time to rejoin Miss Seymour and your parents for the trip back home to the States. Next time you go to Egypt, perhaps you'll get to see the country, you think to yourself.

The End

Glossary

Akhnaton—Known as the "heretic king" of Egypt. When he became the fourth pharaoh of the eighteenth dynasty (1567–1320 B.C.), his name was Amenhotep, which means "Amen is satisfied" (Amen being the chief god of Thebes, the capital of the Egyptian empire). Later, he broke with almost all of the ancient traditions and instituted the worship of the one god, Aton, changing his name to Akhnaton, "He who serves the Aton." His wife was named Nefertiti, and his son-in-law was Tutankhamen.

Alexandria—The chief seaport and second-largest city of Egypt. It stretches along the Mediterranean coast for ten miles and is known for its beautiful beaches. Alexandria was founded by Alexander the Great in 331 B.C. and was originally surrounded by a high wall.

Amen—Also known as Amen-Re (often spelled Amon-Re) when combined with the name of the sun-god, Re. Amen was the chief god of Thebes, the capital of the ancient Egyptian empire, and was regarded as the "king of the gods." Amen was credited with having "created all things."

Anubis—The jackallike deity who conducted the souls of the dead through the underworld to where they would be judged by the chief god, Osiris. If the souls were found wanting, they were devoured by Amemit, the "eater of souls."

Arabic Language—Originally the language of the Arabs of the Arabian Peninsula, it accompanied the spread of the religion of Islam from the country of Iran in the east across the Middle East and North Africa to the Atlantic Ocean. It is now the native tongue of seventy to eighty million people and is understood by many times that number as the sacred language of the Muslim faith.

Aton—The god that Akhnaton tried to promote as the one and only God. Aton was represented by the disc of the sun and was usually shown with rays coming out from it, ending in tiny hands, as if "giving" the life-giving power of the sun to man.

Ba—The ancient Egyptians believed that *ba* was a Godlike element, like the soul, enclosed in the body during life but freed at death. After the *ba* was liberated, it could roam through space, taking any shape it wished.

Beduins—Wandering, pastoral tribes living mostly in the deserts of Arabia, though some live in Egypt and the northern Sahara. They herd sheep, goats, and camels in the desert but migrate from oasis to oasis. The beduins trade for food but consider growing it far beneath their dignity.

Cardamom—A spice plant of the ginger family, highly prized in the Near and Far East. It has a very fragrant aroma and is often an ingredient of curry, a mixture of strong spices.

Carter, Howard—An archeologist who became world famous because of his discovery of Tutankhamen's tomb. He was hired as the chief archeologist for the fifth earl of Carnarvon, who was directing a private excavation in Egypt. Carter and Lord Carnarvon started digging in the Valley of the Kings, and kept at it until they discovered the tomb of Tutankhamen.

Cartouche—An oblong space, enclosed by lines, parallel on the sides and round at the top and bottom, in which royal names were written with hieroglyphs in ancient Egypt.

City of Flowers—The ancient nickname for the city named "The Horizon of Aton," founded by Akhnaton, the "heretic king" of Egypt. One of the most beautiful cities ever built, it vanished back into the desert after Akhnaton's death.

Coptic Christians—At the time of the Arab invasion of Egypt, most of the population was Christian. Under Arab rule, the Copts were gradually reduced from a majority to a minority. The symbol of the symmetrical "Coptic Cross" is very important to the surviving Copts, now about one out of six or seven Egyptians. Its shape is woven into the patterns on the colorful Coptic garments and is often tattooed on the inside of the Copts' right wrists.

Dhow—A two-masted sailing vessel with "lateen," slanting, triangular sails. The large cotton sails when raised look like enormous wings catching the wind. They are "double-enders," the bow and stern both curved into a point, and usually about forty-five feet long. They have no cabins, but small sheds are often built on deck for cooking, etc.

Effendi—A title of respect for an official in Muslim countries. It is often used in the sense that "sir" is used in the West.

Fellahin (sometimes spelled fellaheen)—The peasants, farmers, and other agricultural workers of Egypt and other Arab-speaking countries.

Galabiyas—The traditional long and loose-fitting Egyptian garments that resemble nightgowns.

Hieroglyphs—The seven hundred or so symbols used in ancient Egyptian writing. Some are actual pictures, such as the ones for *bee*, *snake*, *bird*, or *honey*. Others are more abstract—a long oval for *mouth*, a wavy line for *water*. However, only about one hundred were used as actual pictographs; the rest were symbols for sounds or combinations of sounds.

Horus—The ancient Egyptian god who often took the form of a falcon. His left eye was the moon and his right eye the sun. It was believed that all pharaohs were an incarnation of Horus.

Imhotep—A sage, architect, astrologer, and physician, as well as the director of public works and chief minister to King Zoser in the twenty-seventh century B.C. Imhotep instituted the use of limestone blocks for royal buildings and designed vast ceremonial complexes as well as the "step" pyramid at Saqquâra, the first large stone structure in history.

Ka—A kind of invisible double or "guardian angel" of an individual. The *ka* was responsible for life after death, and the body was mummified for its benefit. The tomb statues of the pharaohs were backups for the *ka* in case the mummified body itself was damaged.

Karnak—The northern half of the city of Thebes on the east bank of the Nile. It is the location of the ruins of the great temple of Amen-Re (mentioned above), including the pillared hall built by Ramses I, with its 140 huge columns, some seventy-eight feet high.

Koran—Also spelled Qur'an, is believed by Muslims to be the translation of a sacred tablet preserved in heaven and revealed by the prophet Muhammad. Its basic theme is absolute monotheism, with no divinity except God.

Mediterranean—The sea that separates Europe from the continents of Africa and Asia. It is 2,300 miles from east to west and 1,000 miles wide at its widest point. The Mediterranean connects with the Atlantic Ocean through the Strait of Gibraltar.

Minarets—The towers from which the Muslims are called to prayer five times a day by the muezzins, or criers. The minarets are always connected to a mosque, and the tops have projecting balconies on which the muezzins stand. The minarets symbolize Islam in the way that church steeples symbolize Christianity.

Mosque—The centers of communal worship in Muslim countries. They are designed around a central courtyard which represents the courtyard in the prophet Muhammad's house at Medina where he gave his first sermons. Mosques can also serve as schools, hostels for travelers, and community centers.

Muhammad Ali (1769–1849)—The founder of the dynasty that ruled Egypt from the beginning of the nineteenth century to the middle of the twentieth. Ali, as pasha (governor), achieved absolute rule over Egypt, even though it was nominally part of the Ottoman (Turkish) empire. He improved industry, agriculture, and the lot of the fellahin (see page 121).

Muslims (also spelled Moslems)—Followers of the religion founded by the prophet Muhammad (570–632). Muslims emphasize the worship of Allah (the Arabic name for God). *Muslim* and *Islam* both come from the same

Arabic root, "to submit," in this case meaning "to submit to the will of God."

Nile—At 4,150 miles, the longest river in the world. The Nile starts deep in Africa and flows north to Egypt. It ends in a wide delta and enters the Mediterranean by way of two branches that separate near Cairo.

Omar Khayyám (died about 1123)—A brilliant mathematician, doctor, astronomer, and poet. *Khayyám* means the "tentmaker," the trade practiced by his father. An English poet and translator, Edward FitzGerald (1809–1883), translated some of Khayyám's verses in 1859 under the title of the *Rubáiyát*, or collection.

Osiris—King of the Dead, and chief god of the underworld. In ancient Egypt, from the time a person died, his or her name was prefaced by the name "Osiris."

Piaster (also spelled piastre)—A metal coin, usually of silver, used in a wide range of countries, including Egypt, Turkey, Libya, Syria, and Spain.

Saladin (1137–1193)—The sultan of Egypt who united the Muslims under the banner of "Holy War" and tried to drive the Christian

Crusaders from the Holy Land. Saladin captured Jerusalem in 1187 but never succeeded in driving the crusaders out of a narrow strip of coastline.

Suez Canal—Connects the Mediterranean with the Red Sea. It stretches for 105 miles across low, sandy desert and needs no locks, as the sea level of the Red Sea and the Mediterranean are almost the same.

Tarboosh—In Egypt, at the beginning of the century, officials and civil servants of all kinds usually wore the tarboosh, or "red fez." It denoted that the wearer was a gentleman, or effendi.

Thebes—The capital of the ancient Egyptian empire. The modern town is called Luxor. It is 419 miles south of Cairo and stretches for six miles along the east bank of the Nile.

Tutankhamen—Became king of Egypt upon the death of Akhnaton in the fourteenth century B.C. Under his rule, there was a return to the old religion and artistic styles temporarily thrown out by Akhnaton. The archeologist Howard Carter discovered his tomb in the Valley of the Kings in 1922.

Suggested Reading

If you enjoyed this book, here are some other books on Egypt that you might like:

Brackman, Arnold C. *The Search for the Gold of Tutankamen*. New York: Mason/Charter, 1976. This tells the full story of how Tutankhamen's tomb was finally found by Howard Carter and Lord Carnarvon. It also discusses the controversy surrounding this sensational discovery.

Casson, Lionel, and the editors of Time-Life Books. *Ancient Egypt*. New York: Time-Life Books, 1965. This is part of the "Great Ages of Man" series. It has a clear and well-written text but the emphasis is placed on the illustrations (mostly full page and in color) and their captions.

Chubb, Mary. *Nefertiti Lived Here*. New York: Thomas Y. Crowell Co., 1954. This charming book is out of print but can still be found in many libraries. It is the autobiographical story of a young female archeologist who goes on an expedition to Tell el Amarna in Egypt, once the home of Queen Nefertiti, wife of the pharaoh Akhnaton. Living in a three-thousand-year-old building, restored from Nefertiti's time, the author helps in the excavation of the site. The book also has delightful drawings by one of the other young members of the expedition.

Cottrell, Leonard. *Life Under the Pharaohs.* New York: Holt, Rinehart, and Winston, 1960. This book transports the reader back twenty-two centuries to the colorful era of the "New Kingdom" of ancient Egypt. It describes the household and activities of a "typical" nobleman of the time and vividly recreates what daily life was like under the pharaohs.

Graves, Richard Perceval. *Lawrence of Arabia and His World.* New York: Charles Scribner's Sons, 1976. A simple and lively biography of the fascinating historical figure of Lawrence of Arabia. It is evenly divided between text and illustrations, which makes for easy and enjoyable reading.

Hoving, Thomas. *Tutankhamun, The Untold Story.* New York: Simon & Schuster, 1978. Thomas Hoving is a former head of New York's Metropolitan Museum, where many of the treasures from Tutankhamen's tomb ended up. He relates the story of the discovery of the tomb in fascinating detail and also describes the intrigues, shady dealings, and scandals that surrounded the discovery.

Mendelssohn, Kurt. *The Riddle of the Pyramids.* New York: Praeger, 1974. A thorough history of the origin, evolution, and building of the ancient Egyptian pyramids, this book is well illustrated with line drawings and color photos. It examines the pyramids in great detail and gives an analysis of the many unsolved problems surrounding them.

Ruthven, Malise, and the editors of Time-Life Books. *Cairo.* Amsterdam: Time-Life Books, 1965. This is one volume in the "Great Cities" series by Time-Life Books. It has a large format and the usual dazzling array of color photos that explore all aspects of the city. In addition, the text gives a complete and very readable history of the city, as well as essays on the contemporary scene.

Tompkins, Peter. *Secrets of the Great Pyramid.* New York: Harper & Row, 1971. The "Great Pyramid" is, of course, the one built for the pharaoh Khufu, also known as Cheops. But this book not only examines this pyramid in great (almost exhausting) detail, it also gives the history of all the pyramids on 416 large-format pages. It also contains literally hundreds of black and white illustrations. It is worth thumbing through just to get the scope of the vast amount of information known about the pyramids, as well as the many controversies and undiscovered "secrets" that they still hold.

Vandenberg, Philipp. *The Curse of the Pharaohs.* Philadelphia: J.B. Lippincott Co., 1975. This book analyzes the circumstances of the more than thirty "untimely deaths" associated with the opening of Egyptian tombs, and the "curses" placed upon them. The author gives several remarkable explanations for these deaths and takes the reader on an insightful tour through ancient Egyptian history, customs, medicine, and science.

ABOUT THE AUTHOR

RICHARD BRIGHTFIELD is a graduate of Johns Hopkins University, where he studied biology, psychology, and archeology. For many years he worked as a graphic designer at Columbia University. He has written many books in the Choose Your Own Adventure series, including *Master of Kung Fu, Master of Tae Kwon Do, Hijacked!* and *Master of Karate*. In addition, Mr. Brightfield has coauthored more than a dozen game books with his wife, Glory. The Brightfields and their daughter, Savitri, now live on the coast of southern Florida.

ABOUT THE ILLUSTRATOR

FRANK BOLLE studied at Pratt Institute. He has worked as an illustrator for many national magazines and now creates and draws cartoons for magazines as well. He has also worked in advertising and children's educational materials and has drawn and collaborated on several newspaper comic strips, including *Annie* and *Winnie Winkle*. He has illustrated many books in the Choose Your Own Adventure series, most recently *The Lost Ninja, Daredevil Park, Kidnapped!, The Terrorist Trap, Ghost Train,* and *Magic Master*. A native of Brooklyn Heights, New York, Mr. Bolle now lives and works in Westport, Connecticut.

Follow the adventures of Luke Skywalker, Princess Leia, Han Solo, and the rest of the Rebel Alliance as they battle the evil Galactic Empire!

The beginning of an all-new series of adventure!